RECONSTRUCTION

KARIN AMATMOEKRIM

TRANSLATION BY / *VERTALING DOOR*
SARAH TIMMER HARVEY

Reconstruction
by Karin Amatmoekrim

Translated from the Dutch
by Sarah Timmer Harvey

First published in English
by Strangers Press, Norwich,
(2020 part of UEA Publishing Project)

Printed
by Swallowtail Print, Norwich

All rights reserved
© *Karin Amatmoekrim, 2020*
Translation
© *Sarah Timmer Harvey, 2020,*
mentored by Nancy Forest-Flier

Editorial team
Nathan Hamilton, David Colmer,
Michele Hutchison, Bas Pauw and Victor Schiferli

Editorial assistance
by Senica Maltese

Cover design and typesetting
by Office of Craig

Main body text is set using Arnhem,
Headings are set in Nord

The rights of Karin Amatmoekrim to be identified as the author and Sarah Timmer Harvey to be identified as the translator of this work have been asserted in accordance with the Copyright, Designs and Patents Act, 1988. This booklet is sold subject to the condition that it shall not, by way of trade or otherwise, be lent, resold, hired out, stored in a retrieval system, or otherwise circulated without the publisher's prior consent in any form of binding or cover other than that in which it is published and without a similar condition including this condition being imposed on the subsequent purchaser.

ISBN-13: 978-1911343271

Reconstruction

CONTENTS

CONCRETE	*5*
JACQUES D'OR	*9*
ROOM WITH A VIEW	*15*
THE RADICAL	*17*
RECONSTRUCTION	*27*

strangers press

CONCRETE
(ODE TO THE BIJLMER FLATS)

Royal was how it was supposed to feel. A building that proudly imposed itself, shoulders back, eyes on the horizon. Its feet planted firmly on the ground, indefatigable, reinforced, a protective concrete constant in an uncertain life. And the flats within it carrying a multitude of lives.

Ten storeys underscored by 360-metre galleries; 1600 windows on the street side, and another 1600 windows in which the sun was reflected each day across Amsterdam Zuidoost. And between them were the people. Some wore their lives like tight-fitting jackets, awkwardly and too self-consciously. For others, life was more like a baggy overcoat hanging off their shoulders, they didn't know how to fill all that expectant space.

Royal was the idea. For this reason, the building, along with other blocks of flats, formed a grid-like pattern. One that, if you were to look down at it from high above, would resemble a honeycomb. Honey, from bees; bees who work to serve their queen.

But royal it wasn't. Kings, everyone knows, live in houses made of marble and have little to do with concrete. But if you stripped these flats of their wallpaper, their people, their cheap laminate flooring, and the white tiles in the sober little kitchens, only concrete would remain. But while there was no trace of marble or gold, the block of flats was still a precious thing. It pulsed with life; a satisfied, grieving, excited, aroused, sleepy, buzz between the concrete floors and ceilings, between the 1600 windows that overlooked the street and the other 1600 windows through which the sun peeked as it busied itself, cloaking the park in shadows.

The building began ageing almost as soon as it was completed. Moss and rust took hold, spray cans and indelible pens left their mark. But it kept on standing, supporting the people who climbed it, pissed on it, even scoffed at it. And at least as many people who loved it because of its panoramic views, and because it contained their homes. So, in spite of the piss, the moss, and the daubed expletives, it remained standing. Indefatigable, because it was the rock-solid foundation of all these lives combined.

Take the flat on the ninth floor. Behind the front door with the horsehair doormat and out-of-date children's charity sticker next to the bell, lived a young woman with her two children, back when a tricycle was chained to the drainpipe. She was stubborn and noisy. She could have stared down the devil. The flat supported a couch the mother collapsed onto every time she grew tired of the things that make women tired: men, children, bosses, their own mothers — in this case also bill collectors, social workers; all equally convinced of their own rectitude. Mind, she was also very sure of herself, so they had their work cut out for them. She and her two light brown kids who took turns tearing up and down the gallery on the tricycle, who she loved more than life itself. She was foul-mouthed, but she loved this block of flats. And the block of flats loved her back, because when it stormed outside, the wind whipped around the ninth floor of the building with terrific force. It whistled and moaned and forced itself through the cracks to drown out every thought, every dream the woman could possibly dream in that moment. The children were used to the sounds; they were born inside — during one of those stormy nights, perhaps. They slept through it all, unperturbed. But the mother did not sleep. She crept down deep under her blanket and imagined she could feel the flat sway gently with the strength of the wind. But it stood stronger than ever; feet planted firmly in the ground, proud shoulders, head in the wind. She didn't need to be afraid. It had been built for this. It was loyal.

Still, she'd had to leave. Probably because of the storms, and the elevation. Because, in spite of the elevation, there were always people above her. People who walked around and argued and dropped things, which made her stiffen with anxiety as she sat on the couch. In these moments, the world felt too close. Then, when she looked out the window, into the distance, the other blocks of flats partially visible, and below, the park with its footpaths and its trees and the tiny figures moving through it — then it felt too far away. She couldn't get used to it, so she left. Taking her kids, the tricycle, and everything else, until all that remained was the parquet floor, the white chipboard cabinets in the simple kitchen, and the children's charity sticker next to the bell.

Before long an old woman moved in. She turned the kids' room into a guestroom for her adult son on the off chance he would ever come to sleep in it. Unlike the young woman, she didn't put the couch against the back wall, placing it instead along the short side of the room. She added a wooden rocking chair with a high back beside the window, a TV, a radio, a dark wooden dining table with a crocheted tablecloth. On the first afternoon that the wind picked up again, the flat stood firm. Reinforced feet planted firmly in the ground, head in the wind. The old woman sank into her chair and looked outside, just as she would every day in the late afternoon, when the sun sank behind the buildings in the distance, with the park below and the shadows of the trees growing longer. She poured herself another glass of jenever, satisfied yet a little sad, because of the sinking sun, and the shadows — they make you feel things. The wind pounded fiercely against the windows, forcing itself through the cracks. The old woman took tiny sips of her drink. And the flat faced the wind. Because concrete is loyal.

JACQUES D'OR

There are things you cannot know, things you must be told. Such as the way the baker's street smells deliciously of fresh bread and biscuits, but that the most fragrant place in the camp is actually in the east. That's where the laundries and tailors are, where clouds of steam that smell like flowers and soap hang in the air. I go there every day to watch the men stretch tight bands of clear plastic around the clean laundry and load it onto carts. When the carts are full, they push them through a gate in the wall and then disappear to the other side. Then they return to their shops, while one of them stays behind. He's not one of us. He guards the gate against people like us and does so standing stiffly in heavy boots and a big, white bullet-proof vest with its white bird emblem. His name is Klaasjan, but I call him Classjan because names have a habit of moulding themselves to fit the people who bear them, not the other way around and because I am his friend. He stands stock-still, though he looks like he wants to move but doesn't dare or isn't allowed, which is often the same thing. I feel sorry for him. A person should be free to move around. Even if we cannot leave the camp, I can still decide to either sit here or cross over to another neighbourhood; like the one with all the bakeries, for example.

Classjan carries a gun so big he needs two hands to hold it. I can imagine it's heavy, but I wouldn't ask him if I could carry it even for a minute because that wouldn't be allowed and anyway I don't want to because I've seen what they can do. The first time I went up to talk to him, he shouted I needed to keep my distance, waving the barrel of his gun nervously back and forth. I sat down on a wall a little further up and smiled at him. My father taught me that smiling works like medicine for the heart though it hadn't helped my father very much. Classjan is big, like my father, but his hair looks orange and his cheeks are red. He looks like a boy from a storybook, with his papery skin. And when he talks, he drops the final letters of each word. It's very funny.

'Are you wondering why I'm golden?' I said. I've learned that when it comes to my odd appearance, it's better not to beat around. He didn't react, so I told him I was born this way, but kept quiet about how my father told me I was made of gold because my destiny is to save our people. I said nothing of this because the safe people are afraid of progress and change; it would take away from everything they've done to get this far.

'My name is Kiss-Kiss,' I said.

'Because you're made of gold?' he asked. I knew then that we would be friends. He was clever. I love clever people.

Classjan doesn't talk much. This makes him a good listener. I don't think there are many stories where he comes from. Here, there are more than enough. Some are horrifying, but I don't tell him these. My favourite is one about the calico cat that crosses from the safe side into the camp each morning. He walks casually past the border patrol and all the soldiers know him. He pushes his thick head against their boots, and they bury their fingers in his coat. Then he makes straight for the butchers' street, where he's also well-known. They call him King Calico. Each butcher gives him something to eat. He's become so fat that he waddles more than walks.

Classjan and I are such good friends now that we ask each other questions. For example, he asked if the fat cat sometimes sleeps in the camp. I told him he doesn't. King Calico takes the best from both worlds: meat here, freedom there.

I ask him why the guards wear bullet-proof vests when no one has ever managed to smuggle a weapon into the camp. He says bricks can also do a lot of damage and this isn't a camp; it's a protected village. He says calling our place a camp is an insult to anyone who's ever been in one.

I think of what my father once told us. How twenty years ago no one could have imagined this. How if we had paid more attention to history, we would understand what we're capable of. That didn't seem like the kind of story Classjan was waiting to hear, so I told him different ones instead:

The first story I told him was about how, when I was six, I ate a week's worth of sweet pastel-coloured pills. Contrary to my wish that my baby fat would all turn to muscles of steel, they only made me nauseous. I threw them up onto the bathroom floor and had to explain the little pink mud puddle full of undigested white flecks. Once Father understood his seven-day supply (fourteen pills) was gone, he nearly died right then, of shock. His heart only worked with the pills and the infirmary had a strict policy on how much medicine could be issued to each person. For three days straight, my aunt begged the clinic for more as my father's heart grew weaker by the hour. She didn't get them, because my aunt is already old and still wears a scarf on her head though she knows the safe people despise it. So, my sister had to go. She's sixteen and people say she's beautiful, but when I look at her I see only eyes, and a mouth and a nose, same as everyone else. Anyway, my sister had to go and ask for it. She went late at night even though it was already long past closing time. She came back very late, but she had the pills, and my father recovered. I love my father very much, so I was thankful to my sister.

I took the pills because I'm very short and I'm not all that strong either. I still look six even though I'm already ten; when I was six, I looked four, and so on. That's why it seemed like a good idea. I wanted to shoot up in height. My father ate the same things I did every day, but he was tall, maybe even two metres. The only difference in our diets was those pills, so I thought they were the secret. It was a silly thought. I'm much smarter now I'm ten because I hear a lot, and I remember almost everything. I've also told lots of children they shouldn't swallow pills, so perhaps I've saved some lives. Yes, I've probably saved lives.

The second story was about how I was once named Jacques. My father loved a man with that name, so he named me after him. The other Jacques sang in French. Sometimes my father sang along. It never sounded very good, to be honest. Also, I have golden skin. Not literally twenty-four carat, before you get any ideas about cutting off one of my ears and pawning it. But I *look* like I'm made of gold. I blush and get all warm when I'm in the light, and my skin glistens like something precious. It's strange, I know. People here in the camp used to call me Jacques D'or. The children at the camp school adopted it too but couldn't pronounce it, so they said J'adore instead, which means something like 'I love you'. It didn't take long before they began just making kissing sounds at me, and since everyone likes gold, it seemed like a good name even though it isn't really a name, more of a sound, like kiss-kiss, mwah-mwah. I've learned since that everyone kisses differently, judging from the sounds they make when they imitate it. Sometimes I'm walking the streets and I hear, 'Smack-Smack, how are you?' or 'Chip-Chip, say hi to your sister!' Sometimes they're sounds I can't even copy, let alone write down. Sounds without vowels, sounds that require a facial expression.

In any case, I was once called Jacques, though everyone has long forgotten that name, and I was born with golden skin in a camp I cannot leave. And my mother died immediately after the birth. Some people say she died from the shock of giving birth to a golden child, but my father vehemently denies this. She was already very weak while pregnant. But apparently, she heaved her last sigh when they put me on her breast, and it sounded like a yawn. My father said it was because she was tired, so tired.

The third story I told him was about when I was fourteen months old and beginning to walk. My father called the heads of the camp together: the head doctor, the head teacher, the head butcher, the head imam, the head tobacconist, the head activist, the head philosopher (who was also our neighbour), and the head shopkeeper. Together they decided that for the foreseeable future, my golden skin would have to be hidden from the safe people. While it's true that the safe people had installed countless cameras around the concrete borders of the camp, they seldom patrolled the camp itself and were reluctant to document what was brewing in the little lanes, main streets, and back alleys. The heads told each other this was because life in the streets is too human. The guards don't like to see how much we look like them. They shook their heads, some with sadness, others grimly, and a very small number with resignation, but they all agreed: I must be kept a secret until a big, beautiful plan for my existence could be unfurled. The editor-in-chief of the underground newspaper wrote in a special supplement: *The warm glow of our golden and beloved Kiss-Kiss must be covered by a protective hand that is formed collectively by our community.* He was a little over-the-top, but the people all took his message to heart. Until recently, I had been walking through the camp without a care in the world. Not a single safe person had even suspected the existence of Kiss-Kiss, the golden boy.

The fourth story concerned my father's tendency to speak only in truths. It comforted the people in the camp, and this is why they often came to our house. To the teacher who didn't know what to teach his students because he no longer knew where life in the camp would lead them, my father gave the following advice: 'Tell the children to keep their chins high so that the diamond-studded crowns won't slip from their heads.'

To the teacher's stunned face, he responded, 'Is it not true that the children are our princes and princesses?'

My father knew every question that began with 'Is it not true that...' demanded an affirmative answer, so everything he said had the appearance of truth.

One day I asked what it was that made us so different from the safe people they had to build a wall around us. He answered, 'The only thing that separates us from others is injustice.'

I had to think about that one, but once I understood it, I asked him how he'd come to these answers, and he said the answer to everything was beauty and love. Then he stroked my face. He said, 'Kiss-Kiss, I have a question for you. Do you know where gold comes from? It comes from an exploding star. It isn't made here on earth. Where you come from, aside from my loins and your mother's womb, is one of the few things I do not know.' My father wasn't very modest, as you can see. 'But gold is precious and soft, just like you are. People don't love a thing only because it is precious, but also because it is soft. It should be protected and admired and cherished.'

He was right. The people here do love me. Wherever I go, their faces light up, even if it's only from my skin reflected in their faces and eyes. People think I bring good luck, and since nothing has happened to prove the opposite, this belief grows a little more each day. They kiss me on the head, squeeze my hand, or rub my back in the hope their wishes will come true. And, if their wish isn't answered immediately, they don't get angry, they say instead that Allah's ways are enigmatic, that it is not yet the right time. When they kiss, touch and stroke me, they do it very tenderly, because my father has explained to them how soft I am. And the wishes they whisper in my ear all sound the same because they're for all the things we're lacking here.

I forgot to tell you that my father is also dead. I should have said earlier, but it makes me sad to admit he's no longer here. The fifth story would have been about how, a year ago, after my sister came home and heard the bad news, she spat on the ground and said they were waiting for us to die. 'You too, Smack-Smack,' you too.

My sister is very intense. At night, after curfew, she meets with the other teenagers in our barracks. On these evenings, she talks in truths, just as my father did. She says: 'The people out there have been because their radios are louder than ours, they've gradually come to telling each other stories about danger and safety for years, and believe it.' She says: 'Nobody wants us, neither this country, nor the bread and wash their sheets for peanuts to feel like we're working, they're just waiting until we die. And in the meantime, we bake their from the other side is more likely to grow teeth in his beak than we are to be released. They can't kill us, and they can't get rid of us, so have long forgotten us. The rooster we hear crowing in the morning Those who wait for help will die like my father. The people outside barren fields behind the concrete wall and our plastic barracks. Land of our ancestors. And that is why we have to make do with that we're living.'

My sister pounds her chest and whispers: 'Those who believe in freedom must fight.'

I didn't tell Classjan about my sister. It didn't seem a good idea. But I did tell him the rest of the stories, and he said, 'You're not made of gold, little boy. At best, you're a little yellow.'

I thought about this for a long time. I concluded he would rather think of me as a lie than think of himself as living one. Some lies, as Classjan would say, are safer than others. But we're friends, so both our stories can exist, side-by-side.

This morning, while on my way to the eastern gate, I had a lot of fun imagining what he would think of my new story. About how once there was just a fence where there are now walls and barbed wire. When we looked through the rails of the old fence, we saw people with banners and signs about equality and brotherhood. The people were singing songs. But eventually they left, signs of forgetting already written on their backs. Then the walls were built. Sometimes a song could still be heard on the other side of the wall. Songs with refrains like 'None of us is free if one of us is in chains!' which sounded like it could be true but wasn't. But when I arrived at the gate, everything had changed. In the intervening days, the entrance had been rebuilt. There was no longer a door and the gate had become a narrow, low-lying sluice.

'Where is Classjan?' I asked the men who were busy packing up their stuff.

'Your friend doesn't work here any more. Go home, Kiss-Kiss,' one of them answered.

I was never told anything more. I shuffled over to the spot where Classjan once stood. A surveillance camera now hung beneath a halo of spikes. It wasn't a bad spot, I thought. The sun was falling at just the right angle, warming my face. The wall was a good place to lean against. I watched the men loading sheets onto automated metal carts. When they were done, the last man pushed a button, and the carts began to move. The sluice opened just wide enough to draw in the cables attached to the wagons. Behind the wall, on the safe side, the wagons could still be heard clattering on their rails. It's a deathly sound because wagons have no feelings and no eyes, so they can't have any opinions about us and who we are behind our walls. As I walked away, I heard the camera softly zoom behind me, pivoting sideways. I looked into its cold, dark lens and waved.

ROOM WITH A VIEW

The man I see outside, squatting on the red soil, is related to me. I recognise his concentrated expression, his naked torso, the muscles in his arms and tough, skinny body. The view here isn't alien to me. It is a view that I remember. It's poverty. A simple farmer with a meagre harvest. Skin that's black from working every day in the sun. I see history and no future. And I know who he is because he is a part of me. There is a reflection of myself in the squatting figure, a correspondence. My family is my blood, and I know he knows what I'm thinking. I'm ashamed. Because I know him, and I know he's anything but poor. He is the eldest in a family of eleven siblings. He's respected, both for his age and for the setbacks he's endured. Back in the day, someone once told me, he was the best-looking boy in the village. So handsome that when he married, he left behind a trail of broken hearts. Years later, his wife followed suit and left him for another. He loves her still and is waiting very patiently for her return. He's a lover, a husband. A father, a warrior, a big brother to my mother. The man who looked after me while she was running errands. Who, when I wouldn't stop crying, held me and sat motionless as I mistook his manly chest for my mother's, and sucked on his nipple until I fell asleep. Every time I look up, I catch his gaze. Warm, loving, even understanding, though I don't know how he can understand me or the world in which I move. Today, at seventy-one, he is in the Netherlands for the first time. For a couple of cold, confusing weeks, we run him around on trains and in metros. He even agrees to a ride a rollercoaster. He is sitting beside me now on the couch. Out of habit, he wears plastic flip-flops and with them thick socks to keep out the cold. He speaks three languages fluently, but when we talk, my sentences don't seem to land. His language is warm and slow. Everything I say sounds sharp and hurried. Our conversations are limited to a few words. I believe this is enough. Eating. Being together. For now, no longer separated.

    Far away from here, he lives in a wooden hut built from rough planks and a corrugated iron roof. A bed only just fits inside. Next to it is a small chest, upon which he puts his Koran. There's a shelf above the bed, with photos that curl at the edges. And beside these a row of books. Books I have written. Books that, for this reason, also bear his name. He shows them to everyone who visits. I don't dare to ask if he's read them. My uncle's house is simple but spotless. Outside, there is another small hut containing a barrel of water and a simple toilet. It stands in a yard that he sweeps twice a day with a delicate rake. Under the shadow of the large mango tree are

European flowers he has grown from seeds the family brought him from the Netherlands. In my garden in Amsterdam, he looks around in confusion. A garden restricted to rigid square metres. Lines of plants in pots. Has he ever seen nature so tamed? In his eyes, is this poverty? He runs his fingers through the plants in the children's small vegetable garden. 'Tomato,' he says. I nod. He smiles approvingly. Strawberry. Peach. Cucumber. A single, paltry fruit grows on the apple tree. He weighs it in the palm of his hand. If these apples had grown in the tropics, they would be as big as melons. He doesn't say this, but I can sense it in his eyes. I think of the backyard in his village, where he waits for the woman who left him. He cultivates cassava, avocados, and peppers. His plants are strong and healthy. The sun burns my head and lashes my shoulders, while my uncle moves easily through rows of plants. 'I'm hot,' I say. He hasn't even broken a sweat and smiles indulgently, his battered teeth bared. The front three or four teeth are missing which makes him look old, make him look poor. I picture him mounting his scooter every Saturday to ride the fifty minutes over the dusty roads to the city market. At the crack of dawn, he spreads his produce on a table: cassava and peppers. I visit the market to look for him. He smiles as he spots me in the crowd. A tourist interested in a bit of local colour. Only, he's also a part of me, this man behind the stall, who sells his produce for a couple of pennies. The man squatting on the red earth, concentration in the lines that cross his face. Later, before I leave, I'll discreetly slip him some money. Banknotes in trustworthy, European currency. He'll take it, knowing this is the moment we'll say goodbye. He will ask me if I'll visit him again soon. I'll say I will. When he embraces me, he will hesitate and seem to want to make something clear. Something about death. How it lurks behind memories from the very beginning. I understand, I will want to tell him. I've seen it. And also: 'Don't die. Not until I've had the chance to say goodbye again.'

THE RADICAL

Imagine this: you're a thirty-nine-year-old man.

Your name is Walter. Or no, Martin. That suits you better.

Next month you'll turn forty. You suspect your wife is busy organizing a surprise party. She's very attached to these kinds of milestones. You don't care too much yourself, but you already know that you'll go along with it, you'll look surprised when you enter the room filled with friends and neighbours. Once everyone has gone, you will thank her and try not to be disappointed if she can't convert the party spirit into something more intimate. This is a thought you will want to shake off immediately. Sex has already proven itself to be too much of a stumbling block recently. If you are honest, it has been since the children were born.

You work thirty-eight hours a week in an office located on the outskirts of a medium-sized city in the centre of the country, let's call it Amersfoort. The title on your business card announces you're an account manager, but, if anyone asks about your work, you are happy to explain in detail precisely what your work involves, even if 'I'm an account manager' would be sufficient, since you feel an explanation is what's expected of you.

You have a tall, athletic build. The years have been kind. Your stomach is flat, and your hair is almost as thick as it was twenty years ago. You don't have enough time to exercise intensively, but, on Sunday afternoons, you like to take your racing bike and ride for an hour or so. Except when it's raining, then you stay at home. 'Home' is a semi-detached house you share with your wife and children, two boys, aged six and eight.

The name Martin suits you, because of your long, sharp nose. When you're thinking, you like to stroke the ridge of it with your finger. The little point that protrudes under the skin halfway down reminds you of the bike accident you had as a child, but mostly it just serves as a landmark for your finger. It's often said you have a friendly face. Your eyes are large. When you look in the mirror, they stare back at you, uninhibited. Your mouth is small, yet full. Back in the day, your wife loved to kiss it. You're not dissatisfied with your appearance. You think maybe your hands are your best feature. They're big and manly — even if you're a little too eager to say so. When you grab your wife by the waist, you feel strong.

They say you look like your father. You don't know if this is true. You've never been able to look objectively at your parents. You only see memories. It's different with your wife. When you look at her, you see exactly how she is now, and what she has become. The person she was, what has been lost. And you've been thinking this because of the book you're reading.

Every day you travel by train. The company you work for is located on the square next to Amersfoort train station. The train is a logical choice, and you love making logical choices. The journey takes almost twenty minutes — if there are no delays and you don't have to change trains. You always sit by the window and every day drink a cup of coffee with a splash of milk. What you also do every day, both on the way there and on the way back, is read. Novels. You don't have a strong preference for the literature of any particular country. Instead, you let yourself be led by whatever you feel you need in your life at that moment. Lately, you've had more of a taste for classics, and that's why you sit, in first class, with a book by a Colombian Nobel Prize winner. A first-class season ticket is a luxury you gladly permit yourself, given the chaos that reigns otherwise. It affords a little more peace and a greater chance of a seat by the window, of which you're very fond.

The way you read, your legs crossed, your head leaning ever so slightly against the window, has something feminine about it. You lose yourself in the pages; your fingers touch the paper tenderly, your eyes glide lovingly over the letters. You don't need to look up to see where the train is. The routine of your commute has rusted itself into your mind. Two minutes before the train pulls into your station, you'll close the book and store it between the papers in your bag. But not yet. For now, the story can keep you in its grip. You follow Florentino Ariza as he secretly watches his great love in the reflection of a mirror at the restaurant where he has just settled in for a simple meal. You've never been to South America, but you can taste what Ariza eats. And you see what he sees; the beauty of the woman takes your breath away. Just as Ariza succeeds in purchasing the mirror from the resistant restauranteur, the train nears your station. Reluctantly, you return to your own world. As you join the line of disembarking passengers, you think of two things. Firstly, that it's probably easier to read a morning newspaper than a book. It would make the transition to reality, which causes you to die a tiny bit each day, a little less jarring. To read in this world, instead of leaving it, seems more logical. However, and this brings you to your second thought, a thought that strikes you before you set foot on the railway platform — you don't really care much for reality. You hold the characters in your novels dearer than all the delusions of the day-to-day. What is the purpose of the news, if not to make people feel different from each other? Tax increases, environmental issues, political extremism; topics that force you to form opinions and point fingers. *They* do it their way, but *we* want it our way. While you ask yourself to understand why others think the way they do and to inhabit someone else's mind. Because literature gives you the opportunity to stand in someone else's shoes. Which brings you back to Florentino Ariza as you arrive at the train station's main hall. Kiosks, people, and later, busses pass you by as you cross over to the entrance of the office building where you work. So, Florentino Ariza bought the mirror in which he'd spent the evening watching his true love's reflection. He'd waited his entire life just to be near her. You'd like to be Florentino Ariza. His passion reminds you of what you once shared with your wife — drinking wine together on a red rug in the open air, dancing to the sounds of a street organ in spite of the irritated glances of others. There was a time when you'd look into her eyes, and she'd look into yours, and you both felt blessed. You, a non-believer, had never felt closer to God. Once you were each other's happiness. Neither of you would settle for anything less.

You let this thought slide feebly away. The office requires your attention. Later, at four-fifteen, you're called away from your desk for a drink in honour of your birthday.

'But it's not until next week!' you protest but nevertheless allow a felt hat in the shape of a cake, complete with wobbly candles, to be placed on your head and drain the drinks you are poured, one by one. At a quarter to seven, you call your wife to let her know you'll be a little late. She listens and says, 'Have fun,' before hanging up, and you think you can hear in her voice that she means it. This annoys you. You long for the times she was upset when you came home late because it meant she still liked having you around.

You drink, you talk, and, along with the rest of the men from your department, watch the three interns, who, over-confident from the alcohol, press their bodies together as they dance to music written a decade before they were born. You focus on their slender hips.

A colleague, female, a little younger than you, brown hair, always dressed in an unremarkable white blouse and black pants, comes to stand next to you. She once made a facetious remark in the coffee lounge, which you not without some degree of pleasure went along with. The day after, she'd looked at you just a little too long during a meeting. Since then, you've been sending each other cheeky emails, as she likes to call them. She asks if you'd like something else to drink, and you say, 'Please.' As she walks away to get a bottle of wine, you quickly look around. No one is paying particular attention to either one of you. She returns and gives you a penetrating look.

Her blouse is a little more open than usual. One small breast swells slightly against the white cotton. She feels your gaze and laughs. 'Naughty,' is what she'd say.

'I also have something stronger, if you'd like.'

You ask what she means.

'A drink, to begin with. There's some vodka in our office. Why don't you come with me? All that wine will only make you dull.'

Your first thought is that you can't both leave at the same time. What would people think? She leans toward you. You feel her breasts press against your upper arm.

'I'll go now. You follow in five minutes.' Then she stops. Her strange, sweet perfume forces itself on you. 'Don't think about it too much. I won't either.' Now she's walking away. You watch her go.

Don't think about it too much, you repeat to yourself. Is this the answer? You doubt it. Aren't these the kinds of choices that should be carefully considered, even if they lead to your demise? You think of the books you're reading, of that Flemish novel in which the protagonist, Maarten Seebregs, filled his pockets with bricks and walked into the water at Oostende. Wasn't that a radical yet carefully considered choice? If you decide to go to her and (come on, don't be a pussy, call the beast by its name) have sex, then it needs to be a carefully considered decision. Not something you haven't thought out. Maybe it's because of the exhilaration you got from starting the day with the South American novel, the love of Florentino Ariza, that you ignore your colleague's open-bloused invitation. Maybe the thought of your wife makes you decide to go home. Maybe (and this seems the most plausible reason) you see yourself as a good person, and good people don't cheat. Not long afterwards you are sitting in the train again, now heading in the opposite direction. You're absorbed in your book once more, and a little later, when you get off the train, you can already feel the hangover throbbing behind your eyes.

Days later, your flirty colleague is avoiding you. You haven't yet figured out if she's ashamed of herself or just mad at you. Luckily, you're very busy, and you manage not to think about her. You've finished the novel by the Colombian Nobel Prize winner. Your wife has given you another novel to read.

'A typical women's book,' she said as she handed it over.

In spite of this, you're still interested — you read past gender. Though it is a gruesome story about a slave who kills her child — it doesn't distract you entirely from your recent irritations. Last night, you made advances to your wife in bed. You stroked her back and felt her muscles tense. You didn't let this deter you immediately. After the incident with your colleague, you've been feeling that you have the right to be compensated, so you persisted by pressing your hips against hers. She angrily slapped your hand away and snapped that you shouldn't be so goddamn pushy. You honestly don't understand what you did to deserve such a reaction.

Now it's morning again, and again you're sitting on the train. Your head leans, as always, slightly to the side. Today you're seeking the cool more than the peace of the window. You're reading about Sethe, the slave, and her daughter, now a restless ghost, and you think: *Love can take many forms.*

Your wife said, 'You disgust me,' before kicking the blanket off and leaving for the spare bedroom. But she'd only said that because you had begged her. This is something men should never do, beg for sex. You'd disgust yourself if that were possible. Last night, your love had looked like groveling in the dust, unable to accept the rejection, waiting patiently for the tide to turn.

Sethe, the slave, wraps her hands around the child's neck. They're coming, you think, there's no way out. Sethe's hands squeeze and squeeze. When the beloved child dies, you choke something back. What was that? Were you moved by a book, surrounded by intrepid commuters, at eighty-thirty on a Friday morning? Or might it be the other thought that touches you? The question that keeps pursuing you, growing louder and louder: What is love, anyway? Murdering your child? Being unable to show your husband affection? A marriage devoid of emotion?

You slam the book shut. I'm surprised because this very much goes against your usual routine. It's at least ten minutes before you have to get off the train. You look outside, and there goes your index finger, heading towards the ridge of your nose. You're thinking, deeply and a little feverishly, as if you've caught the scent of something. It's impossible for you to continue reading because a great agitation has possessed you. Love, you're beginning to believe, is a radical thing. Everything you've ever read, every character you've ever inhabited, has followed their thoughts to the ultimate conclusion. Everything they've ever asked of you on paper, you've always done. You've waited your entire life, you've drowned in a cold sea, you've murdered a loved one. What is love, you ask? Love is either radical, or it doesn't exist.

Look, there's the station platform. You stand up. The book is stowed. Do you tap on your briefcase with a satisfied look? Indeed, you do. You seem different to when we first started following you. More decisive, perhaps. Your steps are resilient, purposeful.

You exit the station hall before any of the other passengers. Cross the square. Pass through the sliding glass doors. Traverse the spacious office lobby. The temp at reception watches you as you step into the lift. She notices how tall you truly are. You fail to notice her gaze as you press the number for your floor. The day consists of mundane things. E-mails and, every hour, on the hour, the news on the radio in the corner of your office. Then it's four-thirty. Your suspicion that your wife is throwing you a surprise party has grown stronger over the past week. You decide to go home an hour earlier than you normally would. You find pleasure in the idea of disrupting her plans a little by coming home slightly earlier than expected. This kind of teasing, you say to yourself, is also a form of love.

On the way home, you think of literature and about approaching things in a radically different way. But these are ideas without any clear form.

At home, you take a quick shower and change your clothes. Your wife asks if you wouldn't mind driving to the store, ostensibly for a carton of milk. You take an extra-long time to do this, standing next to the weekly specials and wondering whether you need any cut-price ham.

When you arrive home, the curtains are closed. You open the front door. For a moment, it's pitch-black around you. You have a sudden feeling that you've made a terrible mistake, that there isn't a party after all, but an escaped lunatic has broken into your house, murdered your entire family, and is now waiting in the dark to jump on you and slit your throat too. Then the light goes on, and dozens of people shout 'Surprise!' and you're honestly so startled that you don't need to fake it. There are familiar faces everywhere, a little ill at ease, as people always are at the beginning of a party, thirsty and hoping for an evening full of diversion. You laugh, shake hands, and look for your wife in the crowd. Then she pops up unexpectedly beside you, kisses you on the cheek, and whispers 'happy birthday, sweetheart' in your ear. A couple of people look at you endearingly, the happy couple.

'How nice of you to organise this for him,' you hear someone say. How nice, you find yourself agreeing. Aren't we *nice* together. Your wife walks away to organise snacks, drinks, and fun. You busy yourself shaking hands and receiving gifts. Your children, you understand, are sleeping somewhere else. You're happy that they aren't here. And you don't feel guilty about it.

Later in the evening, you fall into a conversation between your brother-in-law (small and thin, stutters when nervous) and a neighbour (two kids, civil servant). The topic of conversation is The Netherlands-and-its-problems. You listen politely, and it occurs to you they're using buzzwords, employed collectively by the media, as though they had come up with them themselves. What do they think of the 'radicalization of delinquent Moroccan youths'?

'Life-threatening,' your brother-in-law declares.

'A hugely underestimated problem,' your neighbour counters. They're speaking in a tone that suggests a debate, even though they're in complete agreement on every issue. If you pay close attention, you can see their common enemy standing invisibly between them. He is the target of their arguments. You laugh a little because their opinions seem unimportant. Who's listening, anyway? But now and then there are indications of a quick wit, I'll give you that.

'What do you think?' your brother-in-law asks you. His eyes betray his attachment to the topic. His enthusiasm is killing his speech impediment. You're happy for him. You answer that you don't know any Moroccans.

'That's beside the point,' your brother-in-law responds. 'I don't either. And you?'

Your neighbour quickly shakes his head, as if to shed any trace of suspicion.

'What matters is that this society is radicalizing at a rapid pace. These people are beyond all reason.'

You nod indulgently and top up their glasses, while you think to yourself that being beyond all reason sounds quite wonderful. And you feel something, somewhere deep in your thoughts, a premonition perhaps, that wants to tell you you're capable of it too. You could let go of the centre. You could revert to an extreme. You probably wouldn't ignite any bombs or worship any gods. But a goddess, perhaps? You look at your wife on the other side of the room. Your relationship began at an extreme; there was nothing moderate about your love. You were both ecstatic and, yes, radical. Today, you decide with a determination that is starting to suit you better all the time, today you will reclaim what you deserve. Your wife now looks back at you. You raise your glass. Hesitantly, she does the same. Then she does a quarter-turn and starts talking to the people standing next to her.

The last guests don't leave until the early hours. Alcohol has clouded your vision. Now and then, you bump into the repositioned furniture. But you're still wide awake and filled with resolution to do everything differently from now on.

'You go to bed,' your wife says tonelessly, as you stumble over a side table. 'I'll start cleaning up a bit.'

'Are you crazy?' You wave her suggestion away. 'We'll do it together.' You put on a CD: Chaka Khan, an old childhood crush.

While clearing tables and emptying ashtrays, the two of you talk about the party, your friends, the latest gossip. You both laugh!

In the kitchen, she rinses off the glasses, which you put into the dishwasher.

'What time do we have to pick up the kids tomorrow?' you ask.

'Not too late,' she answers vaguely. It's a warning, but you miss it.

'We can sleep in a little bit, right?' Your voice lowers slightly. You look at her face. It has acquired a lot of lines over the past few years — longer lines at the corners of her mouth, tiny ones beside her eyes. Her makeup is smeared and accumulating in the little grooves of her skin. But the Bordeaux she was drinking this evening has coloured the inner ridges of her lips red, and this turns you on more than if her face had been smooth and impeccable. She doesn't give you an answer. This is a second warning. You put a hand around her waist. *Don't hesitate,* you think. Women like decisive men.

'I enjoyed tonight,' you say softly, your lips now at her throat. 'Thank you for the party.'

You kiss the little hairs on her neck. Arousal greets you like an old friend. But then your wife pushes you away, with two hands, which she immediately retracts, as if afraid of burning herself.

'I'm tired, darling. I just want to sleep.'

You look at her, now with fresh eyes, and you think to yourself: Who is this woman?

'We've been doing nothing but sleeping, for... I don't know, a year? How long has it been?'

'Shut up, Martin, stop it!' She slams the dishwasher shut with a bang. 'I don't want to have this discussion every time. Should I do it against my will? Is that what you want?'

You feel yourself deflating, a punctured balloon at a children's party. But you pull yourself together and breathe in new courage. You're practically a new person.

'Goddammit,' you growl, and this alone is enough to spook your wife because you never swear. 'I want what we used to have.'

'That can't happen, we're different now.' She looks at you with a cold stare that you already know too well. 'We are married. *This* is marriage. Deal with it.'

'I don't want a marriage.' You spit this into her face. 'I want love!'

And then, and you hadn't expected this, she shrugs her shoulders, a deadening gesture meant to tell you tough luck, that you'll have to sort it out for yourself, and she turns and starts walking away.

Something in you tears open. It is frightening but freeing, and somehow also delicious and now unavoidable: your rage.

'Stay HERE!' we hear you say with a rolling r as if you were calling a dog, and you pull your wife back.

'Let me go,' she cries, but you don't hear her. You're too acutely aware of her mouth, close to yours, the taste of it as you push your tongue inside, your old friend arousal who returns with remarkable swiftness, her black dress and matching panties, her bare legs. Why does she put in all this effort if she won't give you anything?

Once you've pushed her stomach against the kitchen worktop and pulled up her dress, when you've pushed her with one hand onto the natural stone surface, undone your pants with the other hand, and entered her before realizing what you're doing, when you push back and forth in an almost forgotten motion, you hear nothing but your own thoughts, with every thrust a short phrase: It's not fair. It's my right. It is love. It is love.

And she cries.

You look at your crying wife, panic and disbelief in her eyes. The feeling of triumph has ebbed away on the waves of your orgasm. You lean against the kitchen worktop, dazed, not knowing what to do next.

Would it have been better to turn away a page earlier; to leave Martin to his fate, to be able to say to yourself: This isn't me? It doesn't matter because you kept reading, and you were him when you raped your wife. Do you regret it? Or are you ashamed that you found it so easy to assume his identity?

Let me help you. Turn the page and leave him, the rapist, behind. But enrich yourself with his insights, as you have so many times with the insights other characters have given you (the slave, the suicide, the Colombian lover). Feel free to use them for your own purposes.

Let the radicals run wild on paper, you think — that's where they belong, after all. In your world, the world beyond the page, that is, they're not welcome. All you want is to read your book in peace. On the train. To and from your work. Just turn the page now.

You are safe.

RECONSTRUCTION

That's what it's called. When a city is burnt to the ground after a war has ravaged it and people pull the remains of buildings out of the ground like the roots of a rotten tooth. The city licks its wounds and, with little patience for self-pity, moves forward into the future with new cement, freshly laid concrete, new opportunities for a better life.

They say you identify with the city you live in. If this is true, I am the battered face of my youth. A face that isn't much more than a memory, because the city I grew up in is no longer there.

The concrete behemoths with their weathered windows, little patches of public gardens wedged between pavement and flats, the rosehip bushes, the dog turds, garbage, bin bags blown or thrown off balconies, lost toys under and between the branches of the shrubs — all gone. There was no war, but my old flat on Dennekop Lane has been knocked to the ground. I can't say I loved it. Too many things happened there, and most of it wasn't good. But it was home, and, as people are wont to do, I grew attached. The stories carried inside were fertile soil for a future fascination with people. 'People,' as I once wrote in a novel, 'and their things.'

We lived in the heart of those stories. All I had to do was listen carefully to the easy secrets revealed through the building's cardboard-thin walls. They were secrets pregnant with whispered grief and loss. Was this life? I wondered. Was this what was waiting for us if we dared to grow up? The neighbour who beat his wife, the crying children, the quiet loneliness of single parents, the screaming arguments in which the whole world seemed trapped. Was no one happy in this life?

My mother told me I shouldn't make such a fuss (she meant: Don't let it get to you, everything will be all right), and I searched for examples of how it could be otherwise. I turned to the beautiful, blonde neighbour, with her preference for bad men, who asked me to look after her toddler when they took her out. The delicious, and for me, exotic fragrance of the supper she left for me to feed her child — boiled potatoes with cauliflower and a lovingly mashed meatball. I gave the baby spoonfuls, and when it looked away, I snacked on the meal myself. The mother always returned blushing with happiness, a happiness I meticulously analysed; assessing it, estimating how long it would take for this man to leave her too. How could such a beautiful woman be so unhappy? I asked my mother. She answered that beauty was no guarantee for a happy life. And I thought, then maybe it doesn't exist at all, a guarantee for happiness. Was life constantly stabbing in the dark in the hope of hitting the goddamn bullseye just once?

The neighbour left, and as she got into the borrowed moving van, she said she was going to give it a try somewhere else. Maybe, she added (and in my memory, she looked pensively at the block of flats) it might work out in another place. What she meant was finding happiness.

She left, and everything else in the block of flats remained the same.

On the day a grown man started screaming at the lift, and no one gave a toss, we didn't leave our flats to go and have a look until police cars arrived. Then the sun came out. We stood on the third floor and peered down at the assembled uniforms, at the caution tape being hung in haste, behind that the nosy neighbours, and behind them the hills and the sand that glistened like precious gold between the culms of dune grass. We told each other that it wouldn't be long before the caterpillars would hatch and wrap the shrubs in their white thread, with the creatures themselves, speckled black, standing out against their own backdrop. We hated the caterpillars but loved the dunes.

On that day, with the screaming at the lift and the sun on the dunes, two feet sticking out from under a blanket were shoved into an ambulance. When the ambulance pulled away, the sirens were silent.

That evening, I heard my mother say, to no one in particular, that this was enough. Drug gangs, scores settled in public — it was no place, she said, no place for children. It wasn't long before we also moved away. And we left everything behind, taking only the things we really couldn't do without. All those things fit into two big, old suitcases and the cat's basket.

'Going on holiday?' the bus driver asked. We didn't answer as we boarded. Away from IJmuiden, away from the block of flats. My little brother was the only one who kept looking back. We acted as though we didn't notice his tears.

I grew older, blindly stabbing in the dark for the bullseye, like everyone else. It took years for me to return to the city that saw me grow up. I went back, but never to live there, only ever on the way to somewhere else. Dennekop Lane seemed strangely short. A seaside neighbourhood, smaller than I remembered. The block of flats and its sisters had already been demolished, and they left strange holes in the sky. It felt like war. I turned my car around and drove away, suddenly scared of the memories that peeped, ghostlike, around the corners. Several years later, I returned again. Pretty terraced houses now stand beneath a high heaven. The memories of the flats diminish with each passing day, with each newborn carried across the threshold. Fewer people live there now. There's more space for everyone's dreams.

We are like the city, you and I. We lick our wounds and hope for progress.

nieuw new
dutch **nederlands**
stemmen voices

VERZET is a series of chapbooks showcasing the work of some of the most exciting writers working in Dutch today, published by Strangers Press, part of the UEA Publishing Project.

Each story is beautifully translated and presented as an individual chapbook, with a design inspired by the text in collaboration with The Dutch Foundation for Literature and National Centre for Writing.

1 **RECONSTRUCTION**
   by *Karin Amatmoekrim trans. by Sarah Timmer Harvey*

2 **THANK YOU FOR BEING WITH US**
   by *Thomas Heerma van Voss, trans. by Moshe Gilula*

3 **BERGJE**
   by *Bregje Hofstede trans. by Alice Tetley-Paul*

4 **THE TOURIST BUTCHER**
   by *Jamal Ouariachi trans. by Scott Emblen-Jarrett*

5 **RESIST! IN DEFENCE OF COMMUNISM**
   by *Gustaaf Peek trans. by Brendan Monaghan*

6 **THE DANDY**
   by *Nina Polak trans. by Emma Rault*

7 **SHELTER**
   by *Sanneke van Hassel trans. by Danny Guinan*

8 **SOMETHING HAS TO HAPPEN**
   by *Maartje Wortel trans. by Jozef van der Voort*

Supported by
N National Centre for Writing
N ederlands letterenfonds
dutch foundation for literature

This series was made possible by generous funding from The Dutch Foundation for Literature